Everyone's Hero

The Movie Storybook

By Tracey West

Based on a story by Howard Jonas

PSS!
PRICE STERN SLOAN

PRICE STERN SLOAN
Published by the Penguin Group
Penguin Group (USA) Inc., 375 Hudson Street, New York, New York 10014, U.S.A.
Penguin Group (Canada), 90 Eglinton Avenue East, Suite 700, Toronto, Ontario, Canada M4P 2Y3
(a division of Pearson Penguin Canada Inc.)
Penguin Books Ltd, 80 Strand, London WC2R 0RL, England
Penguin Ireland, 25 St Stephen's Green, Dublin 2, Ireland
(a division of Penguin Books Ltd)
Penguin Group (Australia), 250 Camberwell Road, Camberwell, Victoria 3124, Australia
(a division of Pearson Australia Group Pty Ltd)
Penguin Books India Pvt Ltd, 11 Community Centre, Panchsheel Park, New Delhi - 110 017, India
Penguin Group (NZ), Cnr Airborne and Rosedale Roads, Albany, Auckland 1310, New Zealand
(a division of Pearson New Zealand Ltd)
Penguin Books (South Africa) (Pty) Ltd, 24 Sturdee Avenue, Rosebank, Johannesburg 2196, South Africa

Penguin Books Ltd, Registered Offices:
80 Strand, London WC2R 0RL, England

© 2006 IDT Entertainment, Inc. Used under license by Penguin Young Readers Group.
Published in partnership with and licensed by Major League Baseball Properties, Inc. The Major League Club insignias depicted in this product are
trademarks which are the exclusive property of the respective Major League Baseball Clubs and may not be reproduced without their written consent.
All rights reserved. Published by Price Stern Sloan, a division of Penguin Young Readers Group, 345 Hudson Street,
New York, New York 10014. PSS! is a registered trademark of Penguin Group (USA) Inc. Printed in the U.S.A.

Library of Congress Cataloging-in-Publication Data

West, Tracey, 1965–
Everyone's hero : the movie storybook / by Tracey West.
p. cm.
Summary: With the help of Screwie, a foul-mouthed ball, Yankee Irving must find Babe Ruth's missing bat Darlin'
before the last out of the inning or the New York Yankees will lose the World Series.
ISBN 0-8431-2118-1 (pbk.)
[1. Baseball—Fiction. 2. New York Yankees (Baseball team)—Fiction. 3. Baseballs—Fiction.] I. Title.
PZ7.W51937Evm 2006
[E]—dc22
2006012081
10 9 8 7 6 5 4 3 2 1

My name is Yankee Irving. That's right—my
name is Yankee. My mom and dad are big fans of the
New York Yankees. My dad even works at Yankee
Stadium. He's a janitor there.

I'm a Yankees fan, too. See that guy on TV? That's Babe Ruth. He's the greatest player of all time. When the Yankees played the Chicago Cubs in the 1932 World Series, Babe hit home run after home run. The Yankees were winning the Series three games to zero. It looked like they couldn't lose.

Once, though, I almost gave up on baseball. I liked to play, but I wasn't any good. The guys in the sandlot always picked me last for the team.

I didn't blame them. When I finally got a chance to bat, I struck out.

"You're never playing on my team again!" one kid yelled.

I felt pretty bad. I tried to practice batting with a broom handle and a rock. The rock smashed into an old car. Underneath the car I found a dirty old baseball.

"Guess nobody wants you in the game, either," I told the ball. I took it back to my apartment.

You won't believe what happened next. I was in my bedroom, tearing baseball pictures off of my wall. I didn't want anything to do with baseball anymore. Then I heard the old baseball rolling away. I looked down . . . and it looked back at me! The ball was alive!

"How's it goin'?" the ball asked me.

I was shocked at first. The ball tried to roll away again. But I grabbed him.

I decided to name him Screwie. Then I washed him. Screwie didn't like that too much.

My mom asked me to take supper over to my dad at Yankee Stadium. I took Screwie with me.

"Dad, I found a talking baseball!" I told him.

My dad didn't really believe me. For some reason, Screwie wouldn't talk to anyone but me.

I told my dad about striking out at the sandlot. To cheer me up, Dad took me into the Yankees locker room. He showed me Babe Ruth's baseball bat, nicknamed Darlin'.

"Babe had that custom made three years ago," Dad told me.

"That was the first year he hit fifty home runs," I said. Darlin' was one lucky bat!

Dad left me alone in the locker room so I could look at the bat some more. Then a creepy-looking security guard came in, so I left.

The next morning, I talked to Screwie some more.

"I was in the Majors for two glorious pitches," Screwie told me. "Tragically for me, I was a foul ball. Nobody even came to look for me."

Screwie was a lot like me—he had given up on baseball, too. I thought things looked pretty bad for both of us, but then things got worse. Dad's boss, Mr. Robinson, came to the apartment with a police officer. Mr. Robinson said that somebody had stolen Babe Ruth's bat!

I kind of blurted out that I had seen a creepy security guard when I was in the locker room. My dad got in big trouble for letting me in there. Mr. Robinson fired him!

I felt awful. I just *knew* that the security guard had stolen the bat. Besides, he had looked familiar. I looked through my baseball card collection. Then I found his picture. The security guard was really Lefty Maginnis, a pitcher for the Chicago Cubs.

"Lefty's the biggest cheater who ever stepped on the mound," Screwie said.

I figured it out fast. "Lefty must have stolen the bat so that Babe can't hit! The Yankees will lose the Series!"

I told my dad, but he didn't believe me. He thought I was making up the story, just like he thought I made up the story about Screwie.

I knew what I had to do. I had to get Darlin' back to Babe. Then my dad could get his job back.

"You're never gonna catch Lefty," Screwie said. "He's probably on a train to Chicago by now."

"If we go to Penn Station, we might catch him," I said.

Screwie didn't want to go with me. But we made a deal. If he helped me find Lefty, I would take him back to the sandlot.

We took the subway to Penn Station and got on the train heading to Chicago. Screwie spotted Lefty, and I snuck under Lefty's seat and grabbed the case with Darlin' in it. Then I ran.

Lefty ran after me. The train started to leave the station. I jumped onto another train, but Lefty followed. I jumped onto another train, and Lefty followed me again. Then I jumped back onto the Chicago train.

Lefty tried to follow again—but this time, he didn't make it.

I didn't have a train ticket, so the conductor kicked me off of the train in Pennsylvania. I sat down on a bench and opened up Darlin's case.

"*Aaaaaah!* Put me down! Bandit! Bandit!" Darlin' screamed.

I couldn't believe it. Babe Ruth's bat had come to life!

"No, wait! We're rescuing you!" I told her.

Darlin' calmed down. She asked us to take her to Babe in Chicago. But I wanted to take her to New York so my dad could get his job back.

Before I could get my ticket, I spotted Lefty walking into the train station. I hid.

"Gonna nail him to the side of a barn when I catch that kid," Lefty muttered.

I knew we had to get out of there—fast. I grabbed Darlin' and Screwie and ran off into the woods.

Then, suddenly, a dog sprang out at us—and snatched Screwie!

I chased the dog to an old factory. I got Screwie back (covered in drool) and I met a bunch of guys who were down on their luck. They were listening to the radio, and the news was not good.

"Babe Ruth has struck out!" the announcer cried. "The Cubs may just win the World Series after all."

"I told you Babe needed me," Darlin' whispered.

That changed my mind. The New York train passed by, but I didn't get on it. I had to get to Chicago. If Babe Ruth didn't get Darlin' back, the Yankees would lose the Series.

I headed down the train tracks to Chicago. I was feeling pretty hungry, so I stopped in a town to pick some apples. Then some guys came out of nowhere and took Screwie from me! They tossed him back and forth. I tried, but I couldn't get him back.

Then a girl showed up. She started throwing apples at the bullies.

"Are you going to let a girl fight for you?" one of them asked.

"No, but I'll let her help!" I yelled back.

I started throwing apples at the bullies, but they kept hitting me with apples. I couldn't dodge any of them. The girl, Marti, gave me some pointers.

"Don't look where they're going. You gotta watch where they're starting from," she told me.

It worked! I kept my eyes on the apples. Pretty soon the bullies were begging for mercy. I took back Screwie.

"I was fighting for my life!" Screwie complained.

"Wow, you can really throw," I told Marti. "How did you learn that?"

"My dad pitches for the Cincinnati Tigers," she replied.

I was impressed. Marti took me back to her house and introduced me to her mom. As we looked at pictures of her dad, I told Marti my story.

"My dad can help you," she said. "His team is going on the road tomorrow. They can drop you off in Chicago."

It looked like I could finally stop running. But I didn't know that Marti's mom had called the police. She was trying to help. But she didn't know about Lefty . . .

Lefty pretended to be my dad. He showed up at Marti's house. I ran from him—again. Marti whacked Lefty with more apples, and I got away.

I kept walking, heading toward the stadium where I would find Marti's dad. I was feeling pretty low. I missed my mom and dad. Chicago seemed so far away. And Darlin' and Screwie kept arguing.

Then Darlin' said something that cheered me up.

"You and Babe are a lot alike," she said. "I believe he's going to like meeting you."

I finally made it to the stadium where the Cincinnati Tigers were playing. I met Marti's dad, Lonnie Brewster. He said I could hitch a ride on the team bus.

"Your name's Yankee, huh?" one of the players said. "Your boys lost again last night. Got beat bad. Hate to see them let the Series go to those Cubs."

Even though I was worried about Babe, I had fun on the bus ride. The players all thought Darlin' was a great bat. They played catch with Screwie, too. I think he actually liked it.

The Tigers helped me, too. They showed me how to fix my batting stance.

"You get your feet set right and you can hit anything you can reach," Mr. Brewster said. I tried out my new stance. It felt great!

The Tigers dropped me off in Chicago, in front of the hotel where Babe and the Yankees were staying. I saw a newspaper. The Yankees had lost another game. The Series was tied, 3-3.

Then Babe Ruth himself pulled up in a fancy car! Everyone crowded around him. I couldn't get close to him. I tried to follow him into the dining room, but the snooty restaurant guy wouldn't let me in.

I just *had* to get Darlin' back to Babe! I snuck into the dining room with a crowd of people. It wasn't a great plan. The maître d' saw me and chased me through the dining room. It was a real mess. Finally he caught me and tried to throw me out.

"Hey, bring that kid over here!" Babe called out.

I couldn't believe my luck. Babe thought I was pretty funny.

I blurted out the whole story—about Dad getting fired, Lefty
stealing the bat, everything. Babe just laughed.

"It's true!" I said. "I stole Darlin' back and brought her here."

"Then hand her over," Babe said.

I opened up my backpack—but Darlin' was gone!

Babe thought I was kidding him. I felt awful.

"I'll tell you what, kid," Babe said. "You put Darlin' in my hands, and I'll put you in the World Series. Okay?"

Before I could answer, I saw Lefty sneaking away. He had Darlin'! I ran after him.

But I didn't get far. Lefty pushed me into a car. I couldn't believe who was inside. It was Napoleon Cross, the owner of the Chicago Cubs!

Lefty and Cross took me to Wrigley Field. The final game of the World Series was playing. Lefty was pitching—that was his reward for stealing Darlin'. Cross locked me, Darlin', and Screwie in the owner's box.

"So tragic," Cross said. "It's Babe's last turn at the plate, and he doesn't have his magic bat."

"That's strike three for the Babe! He's really had a tough Series," the announcer cried.

I felt awful. I had failed. The Yankees were going to lose the Series for sure.

Cross left us alone in the box. I was ready to quit. But Screwie wouldn't let me.

"The game's not over, Yankee," he said. "You gotta keep swinging."

Screwie was right. We came up with a plan. I threw Screwie through the glass window. I jumped out of the box, grabbed a banner, and swung onto the field like Tarzan! I ran to the Yankees dugout. Then I handed Darlin' to Babe.

"Sorry I didn't get her to you in time. It's my fault the Yankees are losing," I told Babe.

Babe laughed. "The truth is, we're just in a slump. Darlin' is a great bat, but it's the batter that makes the difference."

The Yankees still had one more chance at bat.

"Who are we going to put in?" the manager wondered. The choice could make or break the game.

Babe smiled. "I know who we're going to put in," he said. He pointed at me. "The kid!"

Nobody could believe it. Not even me. Before I knew what was happening, I found myself at home plate. Babe put Darlin' in my hands. Screwie rolled onto the field, and the catcher threw him to Lefty.

"You can do it, kid," Babe whispered to me.

But I was so nervous. Lefty threw the first pitch, and I swung.

"Strike one!" the umpire yelled.

Lefty threw another pitch. I swung.

"Strike two!"

"You can do it, Yankee!" Darlin' told me.

But I knew I was going to strike out again. I nervously looked around the stands. I was going to disappoint all those people . . .

Then I saw my mom and dad.

It's weird, but I suddenly stopped being nervous. I remembered what Marti had told me about keeping my eye on the ball. I remembered what the Tigers had taught me about my stance. I relaxed. I was ready.

Lefty pitched the ball again.

This time, I hit it!

Screwie went flying! Okay, it wasn't a home run hit. It was a pop fly. But nobody was expecting it. I ran to first base. I ran to second base. I even made it to third base.

Then I ran for home. Lefty had the ball. He tried to beat me home. I ran right over him! Then I dove into home plate.

"It's a home run! A home run! The Yankees win the Series!"

The crowd was cheering, but I didn't really notice. I was too busy hugging my parents.

It was definitely a happy ending. My dad got his job back, with a raise! Darlin' was glad to be back with Babe. Even Screwie was feeling good. He had finally become a home run ball. He decided to stick with me instead of going back to the sandlot.

"It just goes to show you," Screwie said. "You can be the worst player on the field. People can tell you you're no good. They can tell you to give it up. And when they do, you know what you do? You keep on swinging."

And that's just what I did. I kept on swinging. I mean,

how could I give up on baseball?

My name is Yankee, after all!